j   US1708012

Elmer

Anthony's father

ABOUT THE BOOK

Anthony's father doesn't go to the office at eight o'clock every morning like other fathers. He has a more unusual profession. But when Anthony tells his classmates about it, no one believes him. And when he brings a special surprise for Show and Tell, Anthony is the one to be surprised!

Anthony's Father

by

Irene Elmer

Illustrated by George MacClain

G.P. PUTNAM'S SONS · NEW YORK

To
Bret and Dawn

Text copyright © 1972 by Irene Elmer
Illustrations copyright © 1972 by George MacClain
All rights reserved. Published simultaneously in
Canada by Longmans Canada Limited, Toronto.

SBN: GB-399-60741-2
SBN: TR-399-20272-2

Library of Congress Catalog Card Number: 72-149332

PRINTED IN THE UNITED STATES OF AMERICA

04208

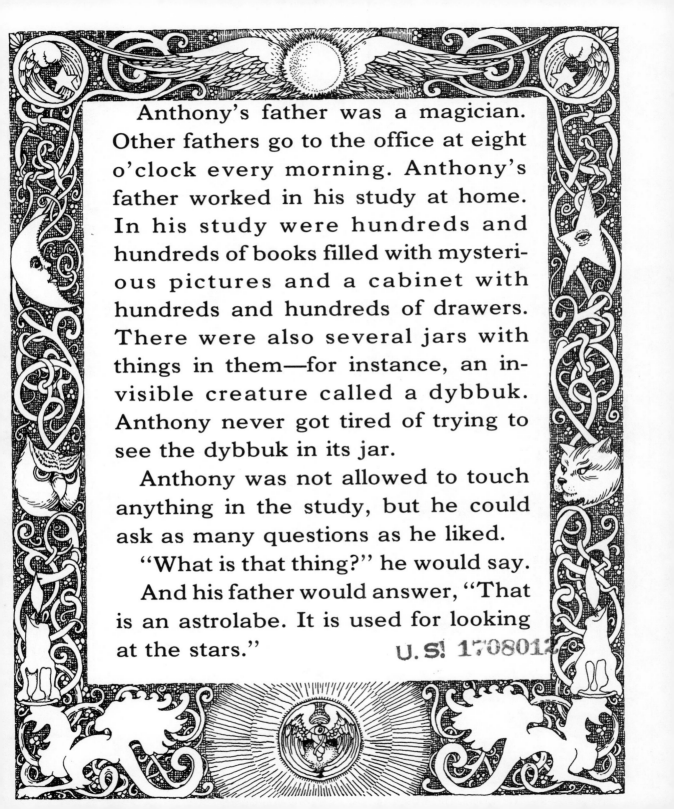

Anthony's father was a magician. Other fathers go to the office at eight o'clock every morning. Anthony's father worked in his study at home. In his study were hundreds and hundreds of books filled with mysterious pictures and a cabinet with hundreds and hundreds of drawers. There were also several jars with things in them—for instance, an invisible creature called a dybbuk. Anthony never got tired of trying to see the dybbuk in its jar.

Anthony was not allowed to touch anything in the study, but he could ask as many questions as he liked.

"What is that thing?" he would say.

And his father would answer, "That is an astrolabe. It is used for looking at the stars."

Anthony's father wore an old black pullover sweater. He had long hands and an iron ring engraved with magic signs. He was very tall. He was very dark. He looked like a magician.

"My father is the most wonderful father in the world," Anthony said. "When I grow up, I am going to be just like him."

Anthony was in first grade. His

teacher was named Miss Fitch. She had curly brown hair and glasses and a nice smile.

One day Miss Fitch asked, "What does each of you want to be when he grows up?"

"I want to be a mother," said Susan.

"I want to drive a bus," said Robert. "My father drives a bus."

"I want to be a doctor," Rosalie said.

Charles said, "I want to go to the office at eight o'clock every morning. My father does that. I want to be like him."

"Those are all good things to be," said Miss Fitch. "What about you, Anthony? What do you want to be when you grow up?"

"I want to be a magician," said Anthony.

"Well," said Miss Fitch. "How nice. Will you do card tricks at parties?"

"No," said Anthony. "That is not what real magicians do."

"Perhaps you will entertain people with shows?"

"No," said Anthony, "but I will have an invisible creature in a jar. My father is a magician, and he has one of those."

"Well, well," said Miss Fitch. "It is fun to use our imaginations, Anthony. You have a very good imagination."

Anthony saw that Miss Fitch did not believe him. She did not believe that someone could do the kinds of things that Anthony's father did.

For a little while Anthony felt hurt. Then he stopped thinking about it, because so many things went on in first grade.

First they planted beans in paper
cups. They covered the beans with
dirt and set the paper cups in the window. Miss Fitch explained how the
beans were going to sprout pretty
soon. Then they drew pictures, and
then it was time to go home.

11

When they left, Miss Fitch said, "Don't forget to bring something to school tomorrow for Show and Tell."

When Anthony got home, his father was in the study. Anthony went in to tell him hello. On his father's desk was a little pile of magical-looking objects.

"What are those things?" Anthony said.

"Those are dragons' teeth," his father told him.

Anthony looked at the dragons' teeth. They were twisted and sharp and smooth, and they glowed a little. "Miss Fitch doesn't believe in magic," he said.

"Not many people do," said Anthony's father.

"If she saw those dragons' teeth, then she'd believe in it."

"Do you think so?" his father said.

Anthony looked at the dragons' teeth. Then he looked at his father. "Could I take one to school for Show and Tell? Just for tomorrow, and then I would bring it back?"

Anthony's father looked thoughtful. "How old are you, Anthony?" he said.

"Six," said Anthony. "Six, going on seven."

"Very well," said his father. "You may take one to school. You are old enough now to learn about the ways of the world."

He chose one of the dragons' teeth and gave it to Anthony. "Don't forget to bring it back," he said. "It would not be a good idea to leave it lying around."

"I will bring it right back," said
Anthony. "I just want to show Miss
Fitch."

It seemed a long time the next day
until Show and Tell.

Susan came first. She said, "I found this sand dollar at the beach. Sand dollar is the real name, but I call this a sand dime, because it's only as big as a dime." Everybody admired Susan's sand dime.

Charles went next. "This is carpenter's chalk," he said. "It's like school chalk, only blue. My father used it to mark with when he built our stereo cabinet. I helped him. Carpenter's chalk makes your hands all blue."

Everybody tried the carpenter's chalk. Charles was right. It did make their hands all blue.

Robert said, "This is a two-dollar bill. They don't make two-dollar bills anymore. Someday it might be worth a lot. The picture on it is of Thomas Jefferson."

Rosalie said, "I have this doll that

my uncle brought me from Mexico. Inside her there is a music box. On her skirt it says MEXICO CITY. She has a real little comb in her hair."

Rosalie wound up a key in the doll's back, and the music box inside played "La Cucaracha."

When it stopped, Miss Fitch said, "Well, Anthony, what about you?

What have you brought us this morning for Show and Tell?"

"I have brought a dragon's tooth," Anthony said.

"A dragon's tooth?" said Miss Fitch. "How exciting! May we see it, Anthony? I have never seen a dragon's tooth."

Nobody else had ever seen a dragon's tooth either. Anthony was very proud to have such an unusual object for Show and Tell. "Dragons' teeth are rare," he explained. "Only magicians have them."

"I see," said Miss Fitch.

Anthony said, "You use them for magic. My father told me some of the ways. For instance, you can plant dragons' teeth and the next day you have dragons. They grow into dragons overnight."

"Thank you, Anthony," said Miss Fitch. "You made up a lovely story. We all enjoyed it. You tell stories very well."

Anthony was surprised and hurt.

"I wasn't telling a story," he said.

Miss Fitch looked serious. "Anthony," she said, "it is fun to imagine things. But we have to remember that what we imagine is not real."

"But," said Anthony, "this dragon's tooth is real."

"It is real," said Miss Fitch. "But it is not a real dragon's tooth. Dragons are imaginary animals. Your dragon's tooth is really something else." She smiled at Anthony. "We really did enjoy your story," she said.

Anthony wanted to cry. But he didn't, because he was six, going on seven.

Anthony wanted to show Miss Fitch. But how? He was watering his bean when he thought of a plan.

I will plant the dragon's tooth, he thought. *And when it grows into a dragon, Miss Fitch will believe me.*

Anthony took the dragon's tooth out of his pocket. It was twisted and sharp and smooth. It glowed faintly in the hollow of his hand. Anthony planted the dragon's tooth in his paper cup full of dirt. He put the cup back on the windowsill next to the others.

Then he went back to his place and sat down.

One part of him felt very good. After she saw a real dragon, Miss Fitch would believe him.

But another part of him felt very bad, because he had promised his father to bring the tooth back. He had promised not to leave it lying around.

But I will bring it back, he thought. *As soon as I have shown Miss Fitch.*

All the same he felt bad all evening. He was afraid his father would ask about the tooth.

But Anthony's father was not like most fathers. He didn't mention the dragon's tooth at all.

That night Anthony dreamed that he went to school and found an enormous dragon, breathing green flames, and that it had eaten Miss Fitch.

Anthony woke up feeling uneasy,

but the sun was shining through his curtains, and outside it was a beautiful day.

And when he got to school, there was no sign of a dragon. Miss Fitch was there, with her nice smile. Everything looked just the same as usual.

Part of Anthony was disappointed, but another part of him was glad. Only a real magician could make the dragon come. It took somebody like his father.

A little boy couldn't do it, Anthony thought.

It was time for a lesson on numbers. Miss Fitch stood up. She turned around and started to write on the blackboard.

Then Anthony saw it. It was gray and very small, and it was climbing up Miss Fitch's back.

It did not look especially dangerous. And it was not breathing flames, only smoking a little.

But it was certainly a real dragon.

Anthony closed his eyes. He hoped he had imagined it, but he knew better. And when he looked again, the dragon was still there.

Miss Fitch said, "Who can tell me what two plus one makes?"

Bravely Anthony raised his hand.

"Yes, Anthony?"

"Miss Fitch," he said, "there is a dragon on your back."

Susan and Robert and Rosalie and Charles all burst out laughing.

Miss Fitch looked serious.

"Anthony," she said, "it is fun to tell stories, but there is a time for everything. Right now it is time for numbers."

"But—"

Anthony stopped. The dragon had crawled over Miss Fitch's shoulder and down her arm.

Thank goodness, Anthony thought. "You can see it now, Miss Fitch," he said. "On your arm."

Miss Fitch looked at her arm. Then

she looked at Anthony. She said, "Anthony, I hope you are not trying to be naughty."

"No, Miss Fitch," Anthony said. "It was only because you didn't believe me about magic. My father is a magician, and I wanted to show you."

Miss Fitch said, "Anthony, that will do for now."

She turned to the blackboard. The dragon clung tightly to her sleeve. *She doesn't see it,* Anthony thought. *She doesn't see it!*

So he couldn't mention the dragon again. When he went home that afternoon, it was sitting on Miss Fitch's desk, steaming gently, its eyes half closed.

The next morning on his way to school Anthony met Robert and Charles. "Seen any dragons, Anthony?" they said. Then they burst out laughing. "Anthony has a pet dragon," they said. "Anthony's father is a magician."

"He is," said Anthony. "He *is*."

But the more he said it, the more Charles and Robert laughed.

One part of Anthony hoped that the dragon would still be there, and that it would have grown enormous, and that it would eat them both. That would show them. But mostly Anthony hoped that the dragon was gone. Because if it was still there, he wouldn't know what to do. And no one would help because no one could see it but him.

When they got to the schoolroom,

Miss Fitch was there, standing out in the hallway with her nice smile. The dragon was there, too, sitting on her shoulder. Anthony's heart sank. *At least it hasn't grown any bigger,* he thought.

Then he noticed an odd thing. The dragon was red.

Anthony felt sure it had been gray yesterday. *Do dragons change color?* he wondered.

"Good morning, Anthony," said Miss Fitch.

"Good morning, Miss Fitch," Anthony said. He tried not to look at the dragon. Its tail was wound like a necklace around her neck.

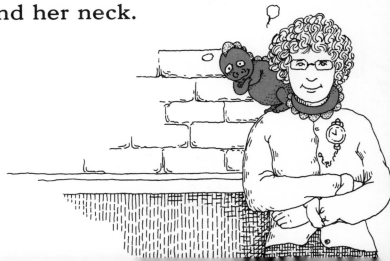

Anthony walked into the schoolroom. A terrible sight met his eyes.

On every shelf and desk and table, on every windowsill, a dragon sat. Dragons chased one another across the floor. There was a dragon in the wastebasket. Dragons flew against the windows, trying to get out.

Some were gray, some pink, some red. There were dozens of them. The smoke from their breaths hung like a fog along the ceiling.

Anthony's legs gave way. He fell into his chair. A dragon scurried out from under his desk.

Anthony closed his eyes. He tried to guess what had happened. Had the first dragon had babies? Or did a dragon's tooth just go on making more and more dragons forever?

There was a loud crash. Anthony opened his eyes. One of the dragons had knocked over a vase.

"Oh, dear," said Miss Fitch. "I must have set that vase too near the edge of the table."

Anthony started to say, "The dragon knocked it over." But he changed his mind. What was the use? He went to help Miss Fitch pick up the spilled flowers.

"Thank you, Anthony," said Miss Fitch. "I am glad to have a good helper like you."

Behind them, a dragon swooped across Miss Fitch's desk, knocking all her papers onto the floor.

Miss Fitch said, "Oh dear, what a wind! We must have left a window open."

Anthony stopped picking up the flowers. He went to pick up the papers.

Two dragons, wrestling together, knocked over a chair.

36

"Well, this is a busy day," said Miss Fitch.

Anthony picked up the chair.

"Thank you, Anthony," said Miss Fitch. "You are doing a good job of straightening up this mess."

Anthony didn't say anything. He knew it was all his fault in the first place.

Luckily after a while all the dragons went into the supply cupboard, where they seemed to have found something interesting. So things quieted down for a bit.

But only for a little while. Presently wisps of smoke came curling out around the supply cupboard door.

"Fire!" cried Robert and Susan and Rosalie and Charles. "Fire, Miss Fitch! There is a fire in the supply cupboard!"

Smoke was pouring out thick and white around the edges of the door.

All the children formed a line, the way they had been taught to do for fire drill, and Miss Fitch led them outside into the playground.

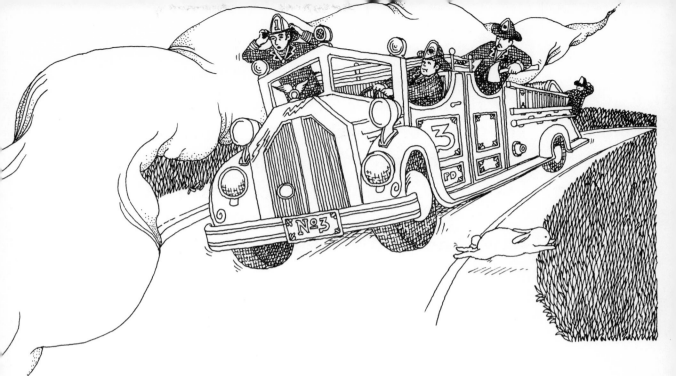

Sirens were heard. A fire truck with flashing lights pulled up. Men in thick black overalls spilled off the fire truck, carrying axes and a hose. They ran inside the school. After a while they came out. They drove away.

Miss Fitch said, "Now we can go back inside. Only the things in the cupboard caught fire. We are lucky. The whole school might have burned down."

All the children hurried inside to see where the fire had been. Only Anthony stayed where he was. "Come along, Anthony," said Miss Fitch. "We must get back to work. We have had a busy day today, haven't we?"

Anthony burst into tears.

"Why, Anthony," Miss Fitch said. "What's the matter?"

She put her arms around Anthony. Anthony buried his face against Miss Fitch.

"It's my fault," he sobbed. "The dragons did it."

Miss Fitch hugged him. "Blow your nose, Anthony," she said. "I am going to telephone your mother. We will ask your mother to take you home. I think you need a little rest. You are all tired out from imagining things."

But it was Anthony's father who
came to pick him up. It was recess
when he arrived. There was nobody
in the schoolroom except Miss Fitch
and Anthony and all the dragons, who
were asleep on the floor.

Anthony's father shook hands with Miss Fitch. On his hand was the iron ring, engraved with secret signs. He was very tall. He was very dark. He looked exactly like a magician.

Miss Fitch said, "So you are Anthony's father. Anthony tells us that you do wonderful things. Sometimes I'm afraid he exaggerates a little. Anthony has such a vivid imagination."

Anthony's father looked at Miss Fitch. Then he looked at the dragons. Then he looked at Anthony. "I see," he said.

"We have had a small fire," said Miss Fitch, "as you may have noticed. I'm afraid the excitement has been too much for Anthony."

Anthony's father looked at the dragons again. The smoke from their breaths hung like a fog along the ceiling. Anthony saw his father's eyes travel around the room until they settled on the row of paper cups beside the window.

"I think he should go home and rest," said Miss Fitch.

Anthony's father looked at Anthony, who was still pink from crying. "Yes," he said. "You are probably right."

He held out his hand to Anthony. Anthony stood up. "Go along, Anthony," he said. "I will catch up with you. I would like to see what sort of things you do in first grade." He walked over to the window. "Here is an interesting-looking project," he said.

Anthony went as far as the door. He waited just outside. He saw his father and Miss Fitch standing together by the window. Miss Fitch was explaining how the class had planted beans in paper cups.

Anthony saw his father pick up one

of the paper cups. As he did so, all the dragons disappeared.

He set the cup down again. His iron ring glinted in the sunlight.

"Child with a vivid imagination," Miss Fitch was saying as she walked Anthony's father to the door.

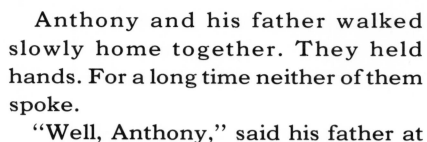

Anthony and his father walked slowly home together. They held hands. For a long time neither of them spoke.

"Well, Anthony," said his father at last. "What have you learned about the ways of the world?"

"People don't see things unless they believe in them."

"That's right," his father said.

They walked on together in silence.

"But the dragons were real," said Anthony finally.

"Oh, yes," his father said. "The dragons were real."

ABOUT THE AUTHOR

Irene Elmer, a native of Portland, Oregon, was graduated from Mills College, and received a master's degree from Smith. For three years she lived in Paris, where she acted as a consultant on British and American speech patterns for Swiss novelist Hans Ruesch. Later she toured the British Isles by motorcycle and traveled in Greece and Yugoslavia. Ms Elmer now lives in Berkeley and is a professional free-lance writer, contributing feature articles to the prizewinning *Northwest Magazine,* writing art reviews, and editing college textbooks. She is also interested in the design, illustration, and history of costume. *Anthony's Father,* based on the story of the sorcerer's apprentice, is her fifth book for young people.

ABOUT THE ARTIST

George MacClain is a talented young newcomer to children's books. He grew up in Philadelphia and was graduated from the Philadelphia College of Art. He is now married and lives on Long Island, where he loves to collect junk and restore old furniture almost as much as illustrating.